© **February, 2020**

Victoria B. Willie & Jaachi Anyatonwu

All Rights Reserved.

No part of this publication may be stored in a retrieval system, or transmitted in any form or by any means, electronic, mechanical, photocopying, recording or otherwise without the permission of the publisher.

For information about permission to reproduce selections from this book, write to *poemifypublishers@gmail.com*

Published in Nigeria by:

POEMIFY
PUBLISHERS

Aba, Abia State, Nigeria.
Tel: (+234)7064982214
http://poemify.com.ng

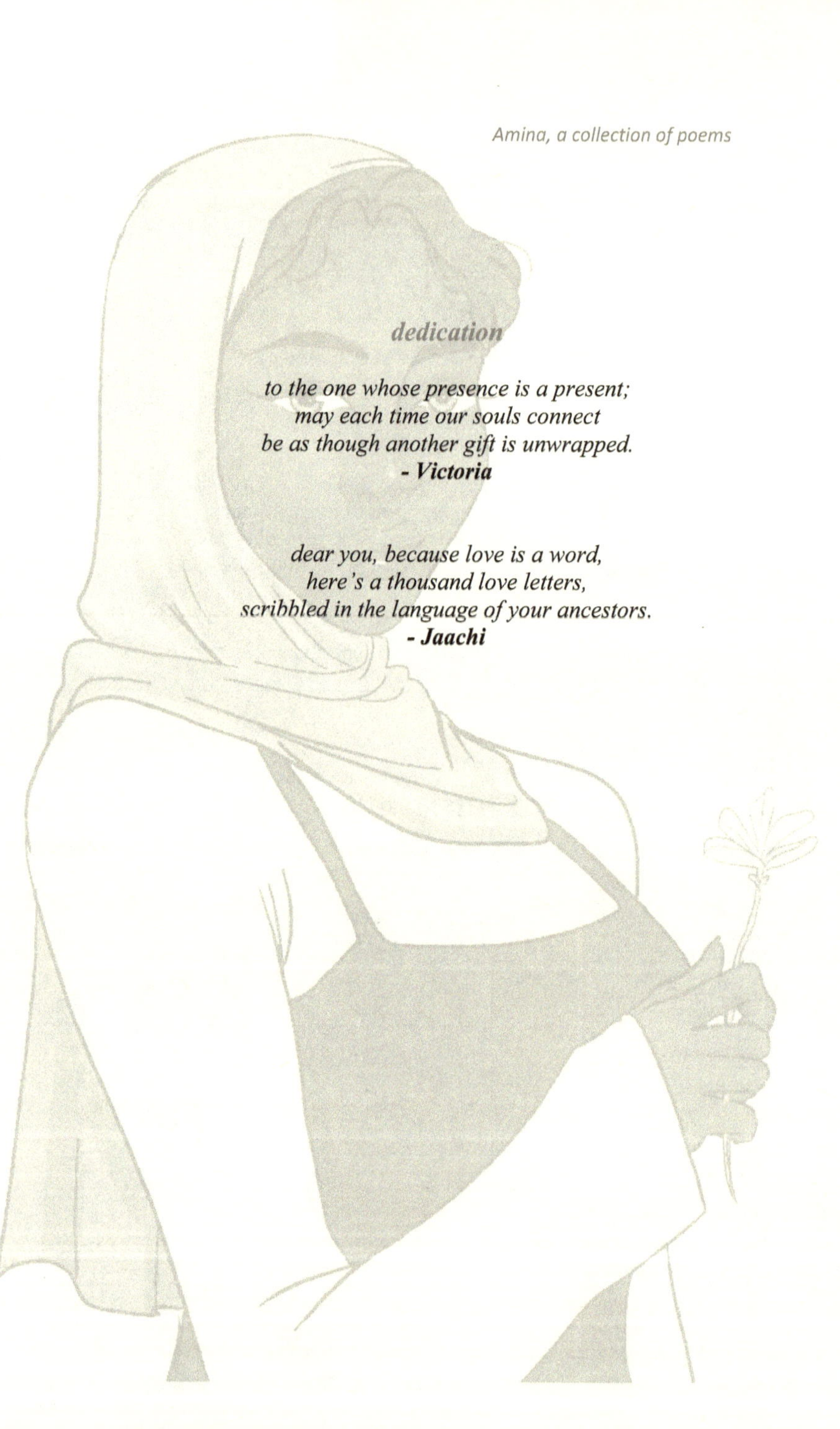

dedication

to the one whose presence is a present;
may each time our souls connect
be as though another gift is unwrapped.
- Victoria

dear you, because love is a word,
here's a thousand love letters,
scribbled in the language of your ancestors.
- Jaachi

TABLE OF CONTENTS

autumn

amina
soon 'twill be autumn
and you shall fall
like autumn leaves
on my waiting arms

also,
    so shall i
        fall
            into the depth
              of you

ali,
when autumn comes
and i fall into your waiting arms

when autumn comes
and you fall into the depth of me

shall we sow seeds of warmth
to keep us when winter creeps in?

daga zuciya na (from my heart)

amina
i do not know how long
it takes a snail to sail upstream.
but i know how long
it takes to sweep sweet memories -
forever.

daga zuciya na
i want to create memories with you
that'll take forever to undo

ali,
forever is not enough
to create and recreate
sweet memories with you

daga zuciya na
i want to create memories with you
that even forever cannot undo

son rise

amina
the glint in your dancing eyes
the bounce of your buxom behind
the sizzling tease of your winks...
hankali fa
insha allah
it must not rise,
this son between my thighs

ali,
if the son rises in the east
it sure will set in the west
na rantse da allah
this son must rise into the heaven
that resides between my thighs

amina, my religion

this passion is best of all
because you make my *imaan* rise
higher than my fears.
i'll opt for you in *dunya*
wallah!
i'll opt for you even in *akhira*.
i say your name in my *du'a*
ina sha'awar ki, amina.

ali,
hear the words i spew forth
for you are the full-stop
that ends all my statements
and you are the answer
to every question my heart chews
masoyina
zuciyata
ina sonki

of wetness & glowing dignity

amina,
i want to do to you
what rainfall does
to a parched soil.

wet

i want to do to you
what sunshine does
to the horizon.

glow

i want to do to you
what crown does
to the queen's head.

dignity

...and most of all,
i want to do to you
what words does to you.

this, i can't yet explain.

of depth, admiration, worship, warmth

ali,

when i'm wet as a humid soil
do to me what a farmer would do

dig

when i glow like the sun-baked horizon
do to me what people would do

admire

when i strut with the dignity of my *hijab*
do to me what subjects would do

worship

and when words elude your lips
i'd do to you what ellipsis would do

cover up

rhetoric

amina,
can you be my change?
i heard it is constant.

can you be my honey?
i heard it never gets sour.

can you be my nothing?
i heard if lasts forever.

ali,
if i be your change,
will you be my balance?

if i be your honey,
will you be my climax?

if i be your nothing,
how long would our forever last?

let me instead, be the mirror you gaze into
to see what tomorrow holds

let me instead, be the duvet you hold on to
when your body craves for warmth

let me instead, be the one you'll never trade for anything,
not even your nothing which lasts forever.

an acrostic for amina

Amina, if i were a poet
Morning and evening
I would write you acoustic lines
Noontime and bedtime
All will end in resounding rhymes

my bank of knowledge

ali, if i were your student
i'd take up your dictionary
and update my vocabulary
with words of pleasure
to describe how sweet, it feels
when you examine my assignment

my bank of knowledge

ali, if i were your student
i'd take up your dictionary
and update my vocabulary
with words of pleasure

pilgrimage to mecca

amina
i want pieces of you like the landscape that surround your
bones.
i want you like the moons that engulf your soul.
these and more you gave
when by *mecca* we came.

i want pieces of your mind engraved in mine.
i want each continent of your flesh pressed against my own.
these and more i got
when by *mecca* we sealed our love.

i want your teeth cutting boundaries of where no one else can
go.
i want my body to be a mecca but only for your own.
these and more i now do own
your body, your mind, your beautiful soul.

i want to spill it all out
the hijab night and caravan kisses
but would they believe
that we had valentine at mecca?
insha allah, i do not lie
every moment spent was bliss.

paradise, we build

ali,
while we dined in mecca
once I met a man
who offered me heaven
even while we still traverse the world

twice I turned him down
many times, I bounced his offer

& said, *"my ali is my all,
my heaven here on earth"*
his emotions not considered.

if I have you
then, I have everything.
your sweet moments, my heaven
your bad times, my hell

if being with you
will lead me to hell,
then take my hand
and let the journey begin

if not being with you
will take me to heaven
come, dear one
let's create our paradise across the sahara

echoes

why wouldn't i render adorations to you every day
when the rhythm of my heart has entangled
with the sound of your moans?

know that i am not uninformed
about the charms that carry your voice waves
on the wings of eternal bonding?

you are she, who command affections
to flow across the length and breadth of the earth
that only the pure in heart could refine.

you are she, who releases signals on a daily
that only the antennas of a heart in sync
could pick them and dance in tune.

how the rumours of our love story
have crossed the seven seas,
the mountain tops
and the woods
into the ears of every damsel downtown

it has swept the ocean floors,
it has wet dry lands,
it has reached the skies,
right now, birds are screaming
and the echoes has touched my heart,
deep

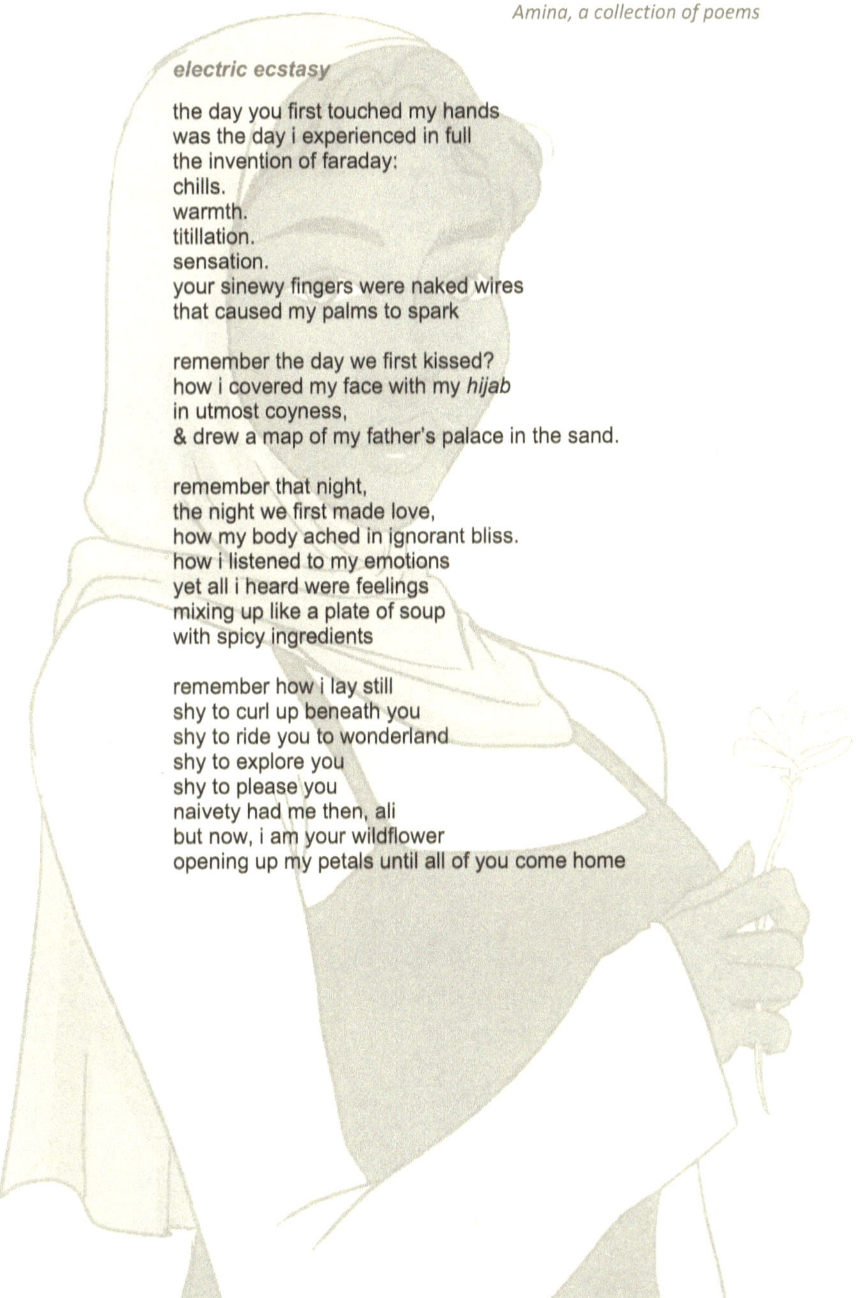

electric ecstasy

the day you first touched my hands
was the day i experienced in full
the invention of faraday:
chills.
warmth.
titillation.
sensation.
your sinewy fingers were naked wires
that caused my palms to spark

remember the day we first kissed?
how i covered my face with my *hijab*
in utmost coyness,
& drew a map of my father's palace in the sand.

remember that night,
the night we first made love,
how my body ached in ignorant bliss.
how i listened to my emotions
yet all i heard were feelings
mixing up like a plate of soup
with spicy ingredients

remember how i lay still
shy to curl up beneath you
shy to ride you to wonderland
shy to explore you
shy to please you
naivety had me then, ali
but now, i am your wildflower
opening up my petals until all of you come home

love is patient – the conversation

ali:
amina, if i rise like the sun
and caress your skin,
will you blush?

amina:
yes

ali:
here i rise,
stimulated by your smiles

amina:
my petals
are dots on your
skin. be quick
rise like the sun.

ali:
if you open your petals
and take me in,
i won't rush
no, i won't rush

a tango for two

amina,
if you fancy me half as good
as i fancy you,
there'll be a tango for two
with roses red,
violets for you,
love a bling,
jingle on the bed

if you need me half as good
as i need you,
there'll be a dinner and table for two
with roses still red
at your doorstep i kneel

if you love me half as good
as i love you,
there'll be a wedding in a week or two
i've got roses red;
will. you. marry. me?

home

ali,
if my morals are at war with the sharia
i would gladly go to the ants
and pick a lesson from them
for a night without the sonorous music
that oozes from your lips
when you lay still in somnolence
is like a night, for a child,
without his mother's singsong voice
lulling him to sleep

should you decide to grow other flowers
i'd still remain in your garden
showering prayers unheard
to *allah*, the controller of hearts,
and the maker of body music
to lead you safely home again
for others shall be mere adventures
whilst i alone am your home

yes, ali
i. will. marry. you.

favourite wine

just one more gulp
of your brew

just one more touch
and i'll melt into you,

amina.

alcohol

just one more taste
of your love

just one more touch
and I'll be drunk in love,

ali.

the lure

amina,
my bed is ready, so is
little johnny

don't be quick to come
i'll last a bit longer
tonight
putting little johnny
to slip.

yours in pun,
ali

ali,
it is always a pleasure
welcoming you down south my cuntryside,

eat as much fruits as you can
but do not forget
to plant seeds for more

yours in pun,
amina

flaws

amina,
like my body, you're my own
i will love you to the moon
and back

because,

your flaws
your snores
i love 'em all.

ali,
you must be mistaken
but i wouldn't mind
for where there is love
the flaws of one
are the flaws of the other

the snores are ours
the flaws are ours
and yes,
i love 'em all

music

amina,
when your voice met mine
we sang our sweetest rhymes
and mirth couldn't last one more night.

ali,
speechless i remain
whenever your words
caress my ears
so now can i just
moan in peace?

amina,
no, you can't just moan in peace
until i have you in one piece

ali,
here I am in one piece
     of meat
eat me
     until you can no more

before, after

amina,
before i met you,
i was toed i'll make no good louvre
in the windows of your heart.
you must be a periventricular contraction,
because you make my heart skip a beat.

after i met you
i knew i'm going tibia okay with you.
you've made a vas deference in my life.
i hope you find this humerus,
dusk to dawn
urine my thoughts.

ali,
i sick understanding
of this recondite knowledge
you just injected
into my head
only then will i be well

if this is sickness, don't get well

this is sickness, ali
the kind of sickness
that requires getting wet
before getting well

dunya

when you
fall into my arms

make sure that your
heart will still be in sync
with paradise,

more than the swelling bliss
of kisses and wet dreams
in this dunya

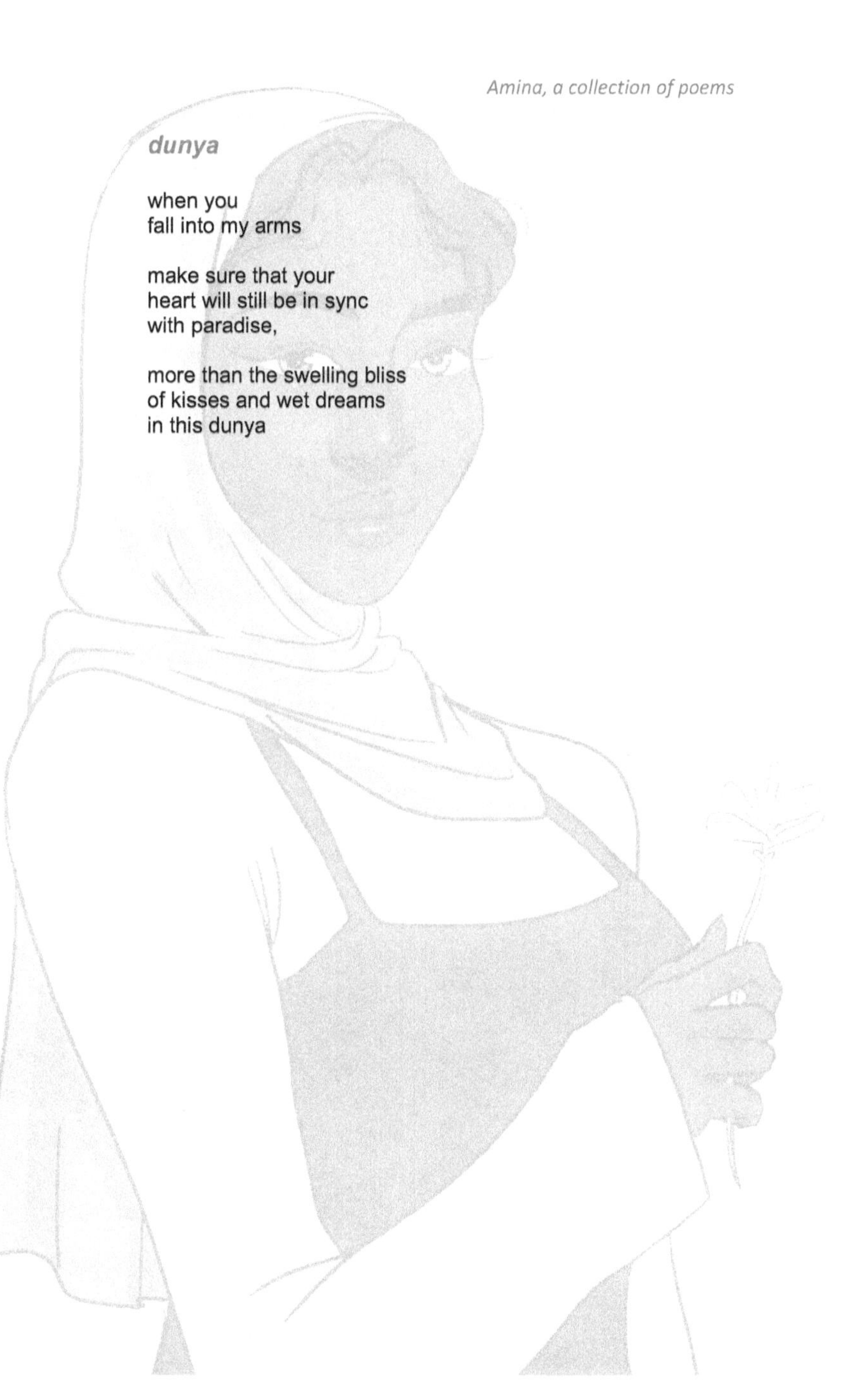

they say, I say

i hear a day may come
when our love would wither

if that day does come
these words we string
these promises we make
as an expression of our emotions
i'd chew and digest, s l o w l y
& carefully.

like an infant
who savours the feel of the food on his milk teeth

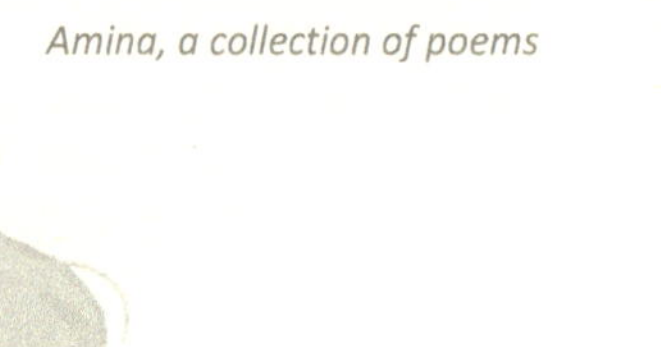

of trees and fruits

amina,
why shake me
from the head
to the heart
to the toe?
there are no fruits on me
i may not fall fruity juices
to quench your thirst

finding & making

ali,
if love can be found
on the body of a man,
let me die
searching for love on your body
while you spend the rest of your life
making sweet love to my body

everything to gain

amina,
i open to *you* like a door
on the hinges of *affection*.
come, lover. come
and make me your home.

your voice is a sun song sung
beside an oasis in the desert,
carried on the wings of an ostrich
into the waiting ears
of a camel. come,
sing a love song to me

i will hold your heart like a
newborn. i hang on
to the hinges of this *affection*
and always, ever
swing open with a welcome song
whenever you come knocking,
in dusk
in dawn
because i have everything to

gain,
nothing

to *lose*

my peace

when I drown in the ocean of longing
let your arms dive in to lift me ashore
to solace
to safety
to life again

you are *my yarima*
maigida
na san ki,
na san zunubanki,
duk da haka
ina kaunarki

if the sun turns its back on the world
i will forever gaze into your eyes
for they light up my world

and if the stars no longer glitter the dark sky
i will make do with your well-crafted dentition
beaming on a platter of an enchanting smile

is it islam or you who are my religion?
it is as though i have found
joy unspeakable
peace everlasting
love pure and holy
in a mere mortal

one everything

one god
one woman
one man
one earth
one pilgrimage
one family
one love

for my overflowing heart

daily, i pray, may allah
guide you to me
no matter how far
with a smile like the sun of the morning
and a gentle touch like the cool breeze of the evening

so, we could become
one everything

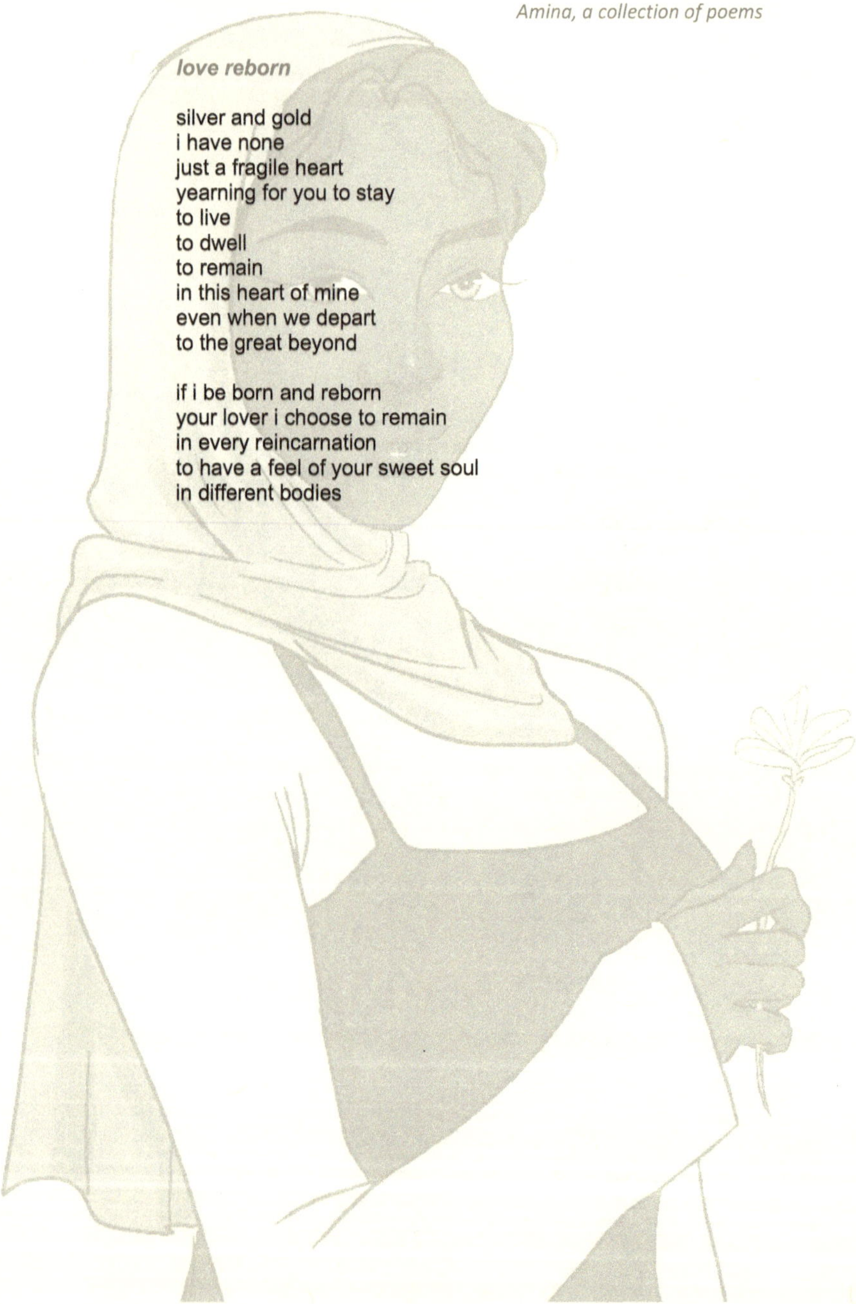

love reborn

silver and gold
i have none
just a fragile heart
yearning for you to stay
to live
to dwell
to remain
in this heart of mine
even when we depart
to the great beyond

if i be born and reborn
your lover i choose to remain
in every reincarnation
to have a feel of your sweet soul
in different bodies

a prayer for you

i pray for you to smile,
amina, to sleep under the watchful eyes of *allah*,
to wake up and see the light
in a warm spring of delight, and feel
the current of *allah*'s love
turning in you like a *water wheel*
as you light up the day, with a smile;
because when you smile i am healed,
a prayer for you
is also a prayer for me.

a prayer for us

i pray for us to stand
when men tremble and fall
i pray for us to give
when men wail in want
i pray for us
to be the reflection
of love in flesh
love blessed by *allah*
shaking the world like an earthquake
i pray for us to live
even when we are no more

paper plane

i fold my memories of you,
craft them into paper wings
leave them to the winds

&
let them fly.

i'll come back to you,
a m i n a
like the northern wind in harmattan

for love, we live

shall we immortalise our story
in lines and stanzas?
for posterity,
shall we?

the world deserves to know
that unlike romeo and juliet,
we live for love

Glossary

Na rantse da Allah - I swear to God
Masoyina -My love
Zuciyata - My heart
Ina sonki - I love you
Yarima - prince
Maigida - husband
Na san ki - I know you
na san zunubanki - I know your sins
duk da haka - I know your heart
ina kaunarki - and I love you

THE AUTHORS

VICTORIA WILLIE

She is a creative writer, a fashion designer and a fashion blogger who believes in the power of imaginations. Born in the late 1990s, Victoria has a Bachelor's Degree in Communication Arts from the University of Uyo and derives pleasure in chasing dreams as that, to her, is the purpose of man's existence —to follow desires through up until they become a part of one's reality.

When she isn't sketching the clothing ideas that saunter into her mind for Ria Kosher, her clothing line, she is scribbling words to describe the imaginations that roam in her mind or writing contents for her virtual fashion magazine, Svelte Magazine.

Some of Victoria's creative works can be found on tushstories.com

JAACHI ANYATONWU

He is a poetprenuer, editor and publisher at Poemify Publishing Inc. Jaachi began his writing adventure as a teenager, gaining unparalleled experience in creative writing, while also establishing himself as a poet. Influenced by writers such as Maya Angelou, Chinua Achebe, Shakespeare, Myles Munroe, Christopher Okigbo, Ben Okri, amongst others, he aspires to quake earth with his quill, while keeping tabs on efficiency, originality, consistency and accuracy.

In 2015, he won the Pengician of the Year Award and in 2016, the Chrysolite Writers Poet of the Year Award. He is the author of many poems and non-fiction, anthologies, self-help manuals and creative writing aides. His works have been published in several print and online publications, including ACEworld Publishers, WRR, AllPoetry, Hello Poetry, Poetry Soup, Poem Hunger, Tush Magazine, and African Writers Magazine. He resides in Aba, Nigeria.

www.ingramcontent.com/pod-product-compliance
Lightning Source LLC
Chambersburg PA
CBHW030416160726
47992CB00007B/3147

9 798630 583246